Iris Grende

DID I EVER TELL YOU ABOUT MY IRISH GREAT GRANDMOTHER?

Illustrated by Tony Ross

HUTCHINSON
London Melbourne Auckland Johannesburg

Copyright © Iris Grender 1981
Copyright © Illustrations Hutchinson Junior Books 1981

First published in 1981 by Hutchinson Children's Books Ltd
An imprint of Century Hutchinson Ltd

Brookmount House, 62–65 Chandos Place
Covent Garden, London WC2N 4NW

Reprinted 1982, 1986

Century Hutchinson Publishing Group (Australia) Pty Ltd
16–22 Church Street, Hawthorn, Melbourne, Victoria 3122

Century Hutchinson Group (NZ) Ltd
32–34 View Road, PO Box 40–086, Glenfield, Auckland 10

Century Hutchinson Group (SA) Pty Ltd
PO Box 337, Bergvlei 2012, South Africa

Set in Baskerville by Bookens, Saffron Walden, Essex

Printed and bound in Great Britain by
Anchor Brendon Ltd, Tiptree, Essex

British Library Cataloguing in Publication Data
Grender, Iris
    Did I ever tell you about my Irish great grandmother?
    I. Title
    823'.914[J]   PZ7

ISBN 0 09 146570 2

DID I EVER TELL YOU . . .

For my five delightful nieces and nephews:
Alan and Ann,
Paul, John and Tina; who, if they are not
all extremely careful, may grow up to be like their
Father, my brother Francis . . . .

About the Most Dangerous Plan We Ever Had?

It was the school summer holiday. Almost all of our friends had gone away. To save us from getting bored our neighbour Mrs Mack asked us if we would like to cut down her hawthorn hedge. It had grown too tall and she wanted it chopped in half.

We worked all day. By the evening our hands were full of small black hawthorn splinters but the hedge was finished. Mrs Mack was very pleased with our work, and next day we helped her make a big bonfire to burn all the twigs and branches. Mrs Mack showed us how to bake potatoes in the ashes of the fire. The potatoes were delicious and it gave us an idea for something to do in our own garden. As it happened it was the most dangerous plan we ever had.

We collected all the spare bean poles we could

find and built ourselves a wigwam. We collected an enormous bundle of dried bracken and wove it in and out of the bean poles. The wigwam was quite dark inside. Then we collected a pile of twigs and made a fire inside the wigwam. My brother Francis had read about scouts rubbing two twigs together to make a fire. We both sat inside the wigwam rubbing away at two twigs until our arms nearly dropped off. We just couldn't seem to make them burn to start the fire.

At last even Francis was quite out of breath and exhausted.

'It doesn't seem to work,' he said. 'There must be something else you have to do.' So he went indoors to borrow the matches, and to get some potatoes to bake in the fire. I waited inside the wigwam just like an Indian squaw. I had to sit with my legs crossed and my head bent down or it touched the wigwam roof. The wigwam was very cramped.

Suddenly our Mother looked in.

'Come out at once,' she shouted. 'You naughty children, whatever do you think you are doing?'

I scrambled out and I couldn't think what was wrong. We hadn't been making a noise at all, and that was what usually made our Mother angry. Francis was shuffling from foot to foot – he always did that when he was in trouble.

'Don't you know that bean poles and bracken catch fire and burn quickly?' she asked angrily. 'You both would have been burned alive. I've never heard of anything so utterly stupid or dangerous.'

We both sat on the back door step and felt miserable. We had forgotten that bean poles and bracken could catch fire and so can children. . . .

After a while our Mother came and said, 'I know what you can do. Light a safe bonfire at the end of the garden, bake some potatoes in that.

Then you can take them into the wigwam to eat.'

So that was what we did. The only trouble was that Francis couldn't wait until they were cooked. So we sat in the wigwam eating horrible half-raw potatoes and trying to pretend that we were enjoying ourselves. Some games can be like that.

About the Cookery Lesson?

After the dangerous plan that failed and eating raw potatoes in our beanpole wigwam I had a terrible tummy-ache. It was still the long school holiday, so our Mother decided to give us a cookery lesson. Francis and I sat on the kitchen floor and searched through all the cookery books to choose a recipe each.

I chose fudge because I loved it. Francis chose gingerbread. He said he hated the taste of it, but was sure it must contain magical properties because of the story of The Gingerbread Man who came alive.

Fudge is easy to cook even the first time. I just slowly melted the butter and sugar together in a saucepan. I stirred and stirred until it had all melted up together. Our Mother kept warning me, 'Mind you don't burn yourself,' and 'Be careful.' So I was mindful and careful and didn't burn myself. It was fascinating when I dropped tiny drops of the hot runny fudge into a dish of cold water. If the tiny drops spread out that meant the fudge wasn't ready. When they stayed together in a lump the fudge was ready to pour into a flat, buttered pan to set.

Francis made a terrible mess with the gingerbread. He made one small mistake, which turned out to be a gigantic disaster.

Francis measured out all the ingredients very carefully. There was one he liked very much called raising powder. We both looked at the tiny pot and read the label. Raising powder looked like fine white salt.

'What does it raise?' Francis asked.

'It puts the bubbles into the mixture,' our Mother answered.

The recipe said, 'Add half a teaspoon of raising

powder.' Francis decided he would like lots of extra bubbles in his gingerbread. So he put in half a teaspoonful; then a whole teaspoonful; then just for luck he tipped in half the pot of raising powder.

Francis thought the raising powder must be the magic ingredient which would make the gingerbread come alive.

He put his dish of gingerbread very carefully into the oven without burning himself. Mother and I didn't know about all the extra raising powder. We cleared up the kitchen while we waited for the fudge to cool and the gingerbread to cook.

Almost at once there was a loud fizzing noise from the oven. Our Mother opened the oven door to look because it was so strange. The gingerbread was going up and up and up – we could see it rising. Our Mother shut the oven door with a puzzled look on her face. Then Francis opened the oven door again. 'Crumbs,' he said, 'Look at this, the gingerbread has reached the roof of the oven.' We both looked.

As we all stood watching the gingerbread gave out a fizzing and whooshing noise. The gingerbread mountain suddenly collapsed and runny liquid gingerbread ran over the edge of the dish, dripping onto the floor of the oven.

'That's proved it,' announced Francis proudly.

'Raising powder really works. You would almost think that gingerbread is alive.'

By this time there was a nasty smell of burning coming from the oven. All the drips were turning into charcoal flavoured with ginger. Some ran out of the oven and dripped down onto the kitchen floor.

Our Mother turned the oven off and whisked the gingerbread into the sink to save some of the mess.

'How much raising powder did you put in?' she asked Francis.

'About half the pot,' Francis answered. 'I think it must be the magic ingredient don't you?' He licked a little of the gingerbread off his finger. 'It tastes absolutely horrible!' he said. We both tasted it too. It was horrible.

We spent the rest of the day scrubbing the oven, the dish and the kitchen floor, which can be quite interesting when you've never done it before.

The fudge was delicious, and I thought I would like to do some more cooking. Francis thought that cooking was a nuisance unless it was on a camp fire, where you didn't need to worry about cleaning up afterwards. But he did offer to be my best customer whenever I made fudge again.

About the Time When We Went to Stay with our Irish Great Grandmother?

We had a letter from our Irish Great Grand-mother, who was our Mother's grandmother. She was immensely old and had writing like fine embroidery. Francis and I tried to read the letter. We could read ordinary joined up writing but we couldn't read this. Our Mother read the letter to us, and this is what it said –

Dear Rose and Ted,
(those are our Mother's and Father's names)
    As it is the long school holiday I think it would be a good idea if Thingummy-Jig and What's-His-Name came to stay for a few days. I could use some help and I would enjoy having them. Write and let me know when they can come.
    All my love, Grandma Conway.

16

'Who are Thingummy-Jig and What's-His-Name?' we both asked.

'That's you two,' replied our Mother. 'Old people can get very absent-minded, you know. Your Irish Great Grandmother can remember many things, but she can't remember names. More often than not she calls people any old thing that comes into her head, or gives them nicknames.

Now, if we let you go to stay with your Irish Great Grandmother you will have to treat it as a working holiday. She will need her hedges trimmed, her paths swept, her shopping done and all her books and treasures dusted. And you must wash yourselves and make your beds

17

without being asked. My Grandmother expects everyone, even two-year-olds, to be sensible.'

It sounded marvellous. We couldn't wait to go to stay with the old lady.

We did our own packing and Francis was in trouble when our Father looked at the things he had packed. Francis's suitcase was so full of toys, books and comics that he couldn't shut it. He had taken out his clean shirts and socks to make more room. Our Father said we wouldn't need any toys or books or comics in our Irish Great Grandmother's house. We would be far too busy, and we would hear more stories in a week than any child was really entitled to. He said 'told' stories from a real live story-teller are a million times better than 'read' stories. He seemed quite sorry that he had to go to work instead of going with us to visit our Mother's Granny.

It was a long bus ride to our Great Grandmother's house. On the way our Mother told us about all the Roses. The story took the whole journey. All the while the bus was stopping to put down and pick up passengers, our Mother was telling us about our Irish Great Grandmother and the Roses.

Our Irish Great Grandmother had been one of a large family. Every time a baby girl was born everyone wanted to call her Rose. Of course it

meant that they had to find as many names with Rose in as they could. There were baby girls baptised Rosemary (just like me), Rosalie, Rosina, Rosalind, Rosamund, Rosanne, Rosetta, Jane-Rose, Mary-Rose and Emily-Rose. The trouble was that everyone had their name shortened to Rose.

'It sounds like a fearful muddle,' interrupted Francis.

'How did the right Rose come when you called Rose?' I asked.

'That was easy,' answered our Mother. 'Everyone had another label as well as Rose. So when someone asked, "Which Rose is coming to tea?"

19

the answer would be, "Cousin Donald's daughter Rose, Rose's baby Rose, Second cousin Rose who lives down the hill, Rose who fell down the stairs, Rose with the sticking out teeth," and even, "Rose with the glasses who lives next door to aunt Rose with the twins." '

'Whew,' exclaimed Francis. 'They sound like a huge bunch of flowers.'

'Don't be surprised,' said Mother, 'if she changes your names while you are staying with her.' We wondered what our new names would be.

We hadn't been staying with our Irish Great Grandmother for very long when she began calling Francis 'Fidgety Francis', because he could never keep still unless he was listening to a story. I loved my new name. The old lady said I was Rose's Little Rosebud, and I should try to be sweet all the time instead of arguing with my brother. I tried really hard, although it's very difficult when your brother is a bossy fidget.

We had a fine working holiday. We washed ourselves without being told and remembered to make our beds every day. We trimmed the hedges, swept the paths, did the shopping and dusted the books. We dusted all the treasures too – but that's another story.

About the Storehouse of Treasure?

Our Irish Great Grandmother's sitting room was a room full of dust and wonder. It was filled on every wall, except where the windows were, with shelves. On the shelves there were treasures from all over the world.

Our Irish Great Grandmother explained to us why she had so many fascinating things. 'Every time someone goes on a trip they bring me a present, and I save them all and never throw anything away. Because there is nothing I need I am not given useful things, I am given things which people think I will like. I always do like them, because they remind me of the giver,' explained Great Grandmother.

'Like that little bird made of seashells?' asked Francis, 'I really do like that. It must be quite precious.'

'Oh, I don't think it's precious in the money

sense,' answered our Great Grandmother. 'If you went to South Wales, as your second cousin Fat Rose With Glasses did, you could buy a little seashell bird for just a few pence. But I like it because it's pretty, and cleverly made, and it reminds me of your second cousin Fat Rose With The Glasses.'

'So nothing here is precious?' asked Francis, looking quite disappointed.

'Wrong,' snapped our Great Grandmother. 'Every thing is precious, but nothing costs very much.'

We gazed around the room at the treasures and wandered along the shelves picking up the ones we wanted to look at more closely. Of course we were very, very careful not to break anything.

Our Irish Great Grandmother sat in her squashy armchair and snoozed. When she woke up I said, 'All the ornaments and all the shelves are very dusty, Great Grandmother. We've both written our names on the edge of one shelf. Why don't we dust everything for you?'

'A wonderful idea,' smiled our Great Grandmother. 'Some of the things could be washed in soapy water. You get a tray and I will tell you which things can be washed and which things can only be dusted.'

We worked for the whole afternoon and didn't

break one of the treasures. There were jugs and jars and pots and dishes. There were dainty dolls dressed up in their national costumes. There were seashells, crystal rocks and several tubes with different coloured sand in them. There was a snowstorm in a jar and a little flowery weather house (which glowed pink for fine weather and blue for the rain and damp). There were boxes of wood, boxes patterned in leather, and a beautiful musical box covered with roses made of china. There was an Eiffel Tower from Paris and a candle from Rome in a tiny golden candlestick. (We were careful to wash the candlestick but not the candle in case it melted.)

At last we had finished with the treasures, so we washed the shelves with some clean soapy water. All the time our Irish Great Grandmother was telling us where the treasures came from and who had given them to her.

By the time everything was back in place we felt as though we had been all over the world.

'Now, sit down and we'll have some tea, my dears,' said our Great Grandmother. 'You've both worked very hard, so either you can each choose one of my treasures to take home, or you can choose to hear a story instead.'

'That's hard,' answered Francis. 'I like both.'

'So do I,' I joined in.

'Well now,' said our Great Grandmother. 'If

you choose a treasure you might lose it, or break it – things do get lost or broken, don't they? If you choose a story it will be yours for ever. It will stay in your head, and you won't have to take care of it.'

It sounded like very good sense so we chose a story, because good stories are treasures just as much as perfect seashells from the beach.

The Story which our Irish Great Grandmother Told Us?

'Now,' began our Irish Great Grandmother. 'Tell me first who you like to hear about in fairy stories?'

That was easy to answer. 'Witches and fairies and dragons and elves and handsome princes and beautiful princesses,' I answered at once.

The old lady smiled a beautiful brown wrinkly smile. 'And you, Francis? Do you like stories about witches and fairies and dragons and elves and handsome princes and beautiful princesses?'

'Well, they are O.K. I suppose,' answered Francis. 'But I like buried treasure, giants and pirates and kings disguised as beggars. I like youngest sons who set out to seek their fortunes, and perhaps best of all I like stories about people who are clever.'

The old lady smiled the old brown wrinkly

smile again. 'Then I believe I have the very story for both of you.' And she began as all the best stories do, with 'Once upon a time . . . .'

We both wriggled down with our legs crossed as though we were making a hole in the carpet. Francis had some hair at the top of his head which was like a palm tree. It always seemed to go even higher when he was concentrating. I noticed his palm tree was listening to the story as eagerly as he was.

'Once upon a time old Ireland was the very land of giants, witches, fairies, elves, beautiful princesses and handsome princes. There were dwarves, dragons, beggars, heroes, vagabonds, tinkers and even pirates who put out to sea in small craft.' (I didn't like the sound of that.)

'But most important in the Emerald Isle of Magic there were the little people.

'There was a time when no one dared to say their name, or it brought down bad luck and great misfortune on the house. The little people are the Leprechauns (don't breathe their name even now). They served their good and honest King Iudan. It was said that the strongest of King Iudan's subjects was so strong he could cut down a thistle in a single stroke.

'Now it was a well-known fact that the little people guarded crocks of gold, which they kept well hidden and buried all over the land. But they weren't just guardians of treasure: they worked at a craft, and most of them worked as shoemakers, which was a fine and honourable craft.

'From top to toe the little people dressed in green. Ireland is a green shamrock-covered land, and they could keep themselves well hidden in a green hedge-row, in the green wood, or in the green meadows. Some were brave and wore red garters, and one famous warrior wore red stockings and earned himself the name of Red-Legs. Wearing red garters became a symbol of good luck. Even unfashionable human farm folk took to wearing red garters to keep up their clumsy woollen stockings.

'Now there was once a clever young farmer

called Patrick. By the greatest good fortune he happened upon a leprechaun sitting on the bough of a tree. Patrick knew he could force the leprechaun to lead him to a crock of gold. But he also knew that he mustn't take his eyes off the leprechaun for a moment or the little man would disappear. It was a well-known fact that Leprechauns could disappear in a wink or a blink or the twinkling of an eye.

' "Look behind you," called the little man. "The bull is out through the gate." But Patrick was both wise and clever and didn't look behind him.

' "Look yonder," called the little man. "The cows are in the oat field." But Patrick was both wise and clever and didn't look yonder.

' "Quick, look in the brook, there's a shoal of fine fat trout." But Patrick was both wise and clever so he didn't look in the brook for the shoal of fine fat trout.

' "Your bees are swarming," called the little man. With that he hopped over the hedge and Patrick followed closely taking good care not to blink or wink. The little man looked sad. He pointed to a bush. "The crock of gold is buried beneath that bush!" Patrick stamped his foot with rage. He had forgotten his spade.

'Now he didn't know what to do. If Patrick took his eyes off the Leprechaun the little man

29

would disappear. If he went back for his spade he would never be able to find the same bush again. Luckily Patrick was a quick-witted fellow. He took off his red garter and hung it on the bush as a sign.

'In less than three minutes Patrick ran home for his spade, and was back again almost in the twinkling of an eye. Of course, the little man had disappeared. And – poor Patrick! – now *every* bush had a bright red garter hanging from it! Patrick dug all day, all week and all the following month, but he never did find the right bush or the crock of gold.

'Just sometimes, as he was digging, he thought he could hear someone chuckling. He was never sure: it might have been the bubbling brook, the

wind gently blowing through the trees, or the rain pattering softly down.

'And that was the end of that.'

'But I like happy endings!' I told our Irish Great Grandmother.

'The very best stories don't have endings,' answered our Great Grandmother. 'And this story does have a happy ending for the leprechaun, and for everyone except Patrick. For the crock of gold is still there, waiting for someone to find it. Though whoever finds it will need to be sharper and brighter than Patrick.'

Francis and I were both certain that if we had lived in Ireland we would have found a crock of gold.

About the Best Toys We Ever Had?

Some of the best toys, the very best toys, aren't made to be toys at all. Torches and magnets are always favourite toys – although they are really made to be tools.

One morning our Irish Great Grandmother sent us round the corner to see the man she called 'Junk Yard Jim'. She told us that he had some special and exciting toys he had been saving for us.

We raced around the corner to the junk yard wondering what the special and exciting toys could be. Junk Yard Jim nodded wisely when we told him who we were and who had sent us. He didn't say a word, but nodded towards the corner of the yard. We walked over to the corner and Francis said, 'He's probably the strong silent type. I've read about them. Lots of muscle but they don't have much to say.' I looked at Junk

Yard Jim but I couldn't see any bulging muscles.

There was nothing in the corner of the yard except five old coach seats. One had the springs sticking out. We felt sure they couldn't be anything to do with the special and exciting toys. So we both began clambering over the piles of junk. It was very disappointing. Everything looked like very plain, and very ordinary, junk. There were twisted up wheels from old bicycles, old tyres, car fenders and vacuum cleaners in bits. Most of the junk was rusty and looked quite useless.

Junk Yard Jim came over to us. He nodded again at the five old coach cushions. 'He means us to stand in the corner and wait, I suppose,' I told Francis. So that was what we did.

Jim went away and began throwing junk about. Some of it he threw into a wheel barrow and some of it he threw into an old dustbin. We waited and waited. After a while Junk Yard Jim looked up from his work. He raised his eyes to heaven, as grown-ups do when they think children are being stupid. He came over to the cushion corner, and picked up the top cushion, which he gave to Francis. Then he picked up the second one in the pile and gave it to me. He still didn't say a single solitary word.

We both stood holding the old coach seats and looking at each other. 'I suppose we had better take them!' said Francis. 'Although I can't think what we are meant to do with them.' So we carried home a cushion each and put them on our Great Grandmother's doorstep. I rang the bell and our Great Grandmother came to the door.

'Put them on the front lawn, my dears, there's more room there than in the back garden, and run back for the other three.'

We carried the other three cushions between us, and took turns at walking backwards because it was awkward and we kept falling over.

We put all five cushions on the front lawn and sat on them piled up one on top of the other.

'Funny sort of toy, if you ask me,' said Francis.

'And not special or exciting,' I added.

Our Irish Great Grandmother opened an upstairs window. 'You are strange children. Aren't you going to play with them? If you spread out the cushions you can bounce from one to another.'

So that was what they were for! They were very special and very exciting. As we bounced up we could see over the hedge. People passing in the street stopped to look and children hung over the gate. In no time at all the garden was filled with bouncing children. Francis had a lovely time

organizing bouncing races. He was a very good bouncer and won most of them.

It started to rain, so we dragged the coach cushions under a tree to keep them dry for another time. All the children went home.

'How did you get on with Junk Yard Jim?' asked our Great Grandmother when we went indoors. 'He doesn't have much to say for himself does he?'

'He doesn't say anything,' we both answered at once.

'Ah, well,' said our Great Grandmother. 'It takes all sorts to make a world. I think Junk Yard Jim must be the strong silent type.'

I tried all the afternoon to be strong and silent like Junk Yard Jim, and not say anything, but that is impossibly difficult as you will find out if you try.

About the Disaster in the Park?

Every morning at our Irish Great Grandmother's we had a big bowl of porridge for breakfast.

It was quite solid when our Irish Great Grandmother poured it into our bowls. She said she had always enjoyed her porridge like that when she had been a child. Great Grandmother showed us how to pour the cream from the top of the milk around the porridge to make an island. And then as we ate it we channelled out little tributaries and made ponds and lakes where the milk ran through like tiny rivers. After eating about half way through the porridge there would be large lakes of milk and several islands. It was most interesting deciding which pond to drink or which island to eat and all the time making the rivers wider and wider.

One morning the sun was shining brightly and our Irish Great Grandmother told us that today we would be explorers. First we needed a map and a list of provisions. Great Grandmother drew a simple map. We could make a list of provisions, which we would buy at the shops on the way to the park. The map showed the shops and the park which we would explore and where we would eat our provisions. (Saying we were going to be explorers was only a grand way of saying we were going for a picnic really).

We put on the list: two packets of crisps, two apples, two bread rolls and some cheese. Our Irish Great Grandmother gave us the list and some money and we set off, carefully following the map because we had never been there before.

We stopped at the first shop on our map. 'You know what explorers really eat don't you?' asked Francis. 'They catch fish where they can, and have packets of chocolate because there's plenty of energy in chocolate.'

'What's energy?' I asked.

'It's what makes you strong and keeps you going,' answered Francis.

Well I did like chocolate more than bread rolls or apples or crisps or cheese, so we decided to spend all the money for provisions on chocolate, and our pocket money as well.

We didn't go into the shop on our Great Grandmother's map, we went to the sweet shop instead. We bought loads of different kinds of chocolate. We bought milk chocolate, plain chocolate, hundreds and thousands, chocolate drops and two munchy bars, chocolate-covered peanuts and raisins and a very small box of chocolates because I liked the picture on the box. We bought two bottles of fizzy lemonade as well.

We followed the map to the park and sat on a bench to eat some of the chocolate to give us energy.

'We must keep eating the chocolate,' said Francis, 'or we shall starve – that's what explorers do.' So we kept eating the chocolate to keep ourselves from starving.

On the way across the park we turned upside down several times on the bar which was built across the footpath to keep bicycles out. While we were hanging by our knees, I said to Francis, 'I think I've had enough chocolate to last me forever – you can eat all the rest.'

Then we drank our fizzy drinks and I went on onc of the swings. Francis sat on the grass and ate some more chocolate to keep himself from starving.

The park had a splendid slide. Our Great Grandmother had drawn it on the map for us. I went up first and Francis climbed slowly behind me. 'Whoosh' I flew down to the bottom. Francis sat quite still at the top.

'Not scared are you?' I asked him.

'No, I just feel funny.' I noticed his face was a greenish colour. Then quite unexpectedly and quite surprisingly Francis was sick right down the slide.

He sat at the top of the slide and stared down at the horrible mess. Then he turned and climbed back down the steps. Then we both stood and gazed at the horrible mess, not knowing what to do about it.

'I think we should go back to Great Grandmother's house,' said Francis. So we went back and told her all about the exploring and the chocolate and the mess on the slide.

'Fill a whatsaname with some what-d'you-call-it,' said Great Grandmother. 'We must go and wash the thingummy before anyone slides through it.'

So I filled a bucket (which of course was a whatsaname) with some water and disinfectant (which of course was some what-d'you-call-it). We carried the bucket carefully between us down to the park. I climbed up to the top and washed the top of the slide, and Great Grandmother washed the bottom.

The slide was soon clean again but it didn't look shiny any more. 'Try a slide down it,' said Great Grandmother. But the slide was damp and had lost its slipperiness. 'Never mind,' said Great Grandmother, 'When it's quite dry other children will come and slide on it and soon all the sliding children will make it slippery again.'

Back at Great Grandmother's house Francis was looking better.

'That will teach you both a lesson,' said Great Grandmother. 'Too much chocolate is no good for explorers or anyone else.'

'Anyway,' answered Francis, 'I think there was something wrong with the fizzy pop. It had too many bubbles in it. It was enough to make any explorer explode.'

'Draw me a picture of an exploding explorer,' suggested our Great Grandmother.

42

Francis did just that and I sat and watched with my shoes and socks off because they were soaking wet: I had spilled some of the water as I carried the bucket up the slide in the park.

About Trying to Mind the Terrible Two-Year-Old?

In the house next to our Irish Great Grandmother's house lived a very nice family. The father, Mr Turner, was a policeman and went off to the Police Station every morning looking very smart in his uniform. The Mother, Mrs Turner, was very pretty. She had a glorious mop of beautiful red curls. Mrs Turner stayed at home to look after the house and their little daughter.

Our Irish Great Grandmother called Mr Turner 'the bright young bobby', and she called Mrs Turner 'the pocket Venus' because she was small and beautiful. She called the little girl Topsy-Turvey because our Great Grandmother said she was always upside down.

We were sure that no-one could really be called Topsy-Turvey Turner because it sounded quite crazy. We waited to discover what the little

45

girl's name really was. It wasn't long before we found out.

One sunny afternoon our Irish Great Grandmother suggested that we should go next door to mind Topsy-Turvey. 'You could take her into the garden and teach her something,' suggested our Great Grandmother.

'I could show her how to make a bonfire safely,' suggested Francis.

'And I could show her how to make cats' cradles,' I joined in.

'No, no, no!' gasped our Great Grandmother, 'that's all much too difficult. Help her to find an ants' nest to watch or help her to dig the garden. Read her some rhymes and stories from her books. You might teach her to go head over heels so long as you teach her to tuck her head properly.'

We rushed next door and rang the bell. Mrs

Turner, the pocket Venus, was expecting us. We did the things our Great Grandmother had suggested. Topsy-Turvey was very good and showed us how pleased she was by chattering and chuckling all the time. We enjoyed ourselves too. We both felt very grand and grown-up because we knew lots of things that Topsy-Turvey Turner didn't.

After we had played for a while Mrs Turner came into the garden with some drinks of orange and a plate of biscuits. Topsy-Turvey picked up the whole plate of biscuits and tipped them over her head.

'Oh dear,' sighed her mother, 'she does get so excited.'

We all helped to pick up the biscuits.

'What is her real name?' I asked. 'Topsy-Turvey can't really be called Topsy-Turvey can she?'

Mrs Turner smiled. 'Well, since your Great Grandmother first called her Topsy-Turvey we have hardly ever used her real name. It does seem to suit her so well. Her real name is Sophia-Jane. Sophia means wise. Perhaps Sophia-Jane will grow up to be wise when she stops being so Topsy-Turvey.'

Mrs Turner asked us if we would like to water the garden. All children like watering gardens on sunny days and we said we would love to. We took turns at holding the hose and letting Topsy-Turvey help. When we had nearly finished Francis said, 'I think Topsy-Turvey could do some all by herself.' We showed Topsy-Turvey how to water the flowers by the back door and stood well away to let her feel grown-up and clever.

But Topsy-Turvey wasn't to be trusted with the hose-pipe. She started to water the path, the back door and the kitchen windows. Francis ran towards her to take the hose away and Topsy-Turvey watered him, very thoroughly. He ran down the garden out of range. I tried and Topsy-Turvey hosed me down too, laughing her little head off.

'Let's both try,' suggested Francis, so we both ran and Topsy-Turvey hosed us both down again.

Mrs Turner looked out to see what was making us all laugh so loudly. 'I will creep out of the kitchen door and turn off the garden tap,' she called.

Topsy-Turvey heard the kitchen door open and turned the hose-pipe on her Mother – who ran back inside laughing and not looking so beautiful any more, just wet.

We simply didn't know how to stop Topsy-Turvey. In the end Francis ran up the garden and turned off the tap. Topsy-Turvey nearly

drowned him while he was doing it. As soon as the water stopped running Topsy-Turvey burst into tears. I knew she would. She had been having such a lovely time.

Mr Turner and our Great Grandmother laughed when they saw how wet we all were. 'Two-year-olds are always terrible,' said our Great Grandmother. 'They pretend they can't understand a word you say, unless it suits them.'

'You're a brave lad, Francis,' said Mr Turner. 'You're braver than I am. I wouldn't go near Topsy-Turvey with a hose-pipe in her hand. I'm not afraid of bank robbers or burglars – but Topsy-Turvey with a running hose-pipe would frighten me to death. You'd make a good policeman.'

Francis puffed out his chest and looked very proud of himself.

Topsy-Turvey pointed to the garden tap and said, 'Water, more, more, more.'

'We've all had enough water for one day, thank you, Miss,' said Mr Turner. He hoisted Topsy-Turvey over his shoulder and carried her upstairs to the bathroom for her nice warm bath. So she did get some more water to play with that day, after all.

About the Nest of Mice?

It was pouring with rain. Not tiny misty drops of rain which feel cool and soft, but great dollops of huge rain-drops which soaked you right through in a moment.

Francis and I both went to get our wellington boots from the cupboard under the stairs. It hadn't rained for a long time and the boots seemed to have been pushed right to the back. Francis soon found both of his and I found one of mine. Then the search began, because one wellington boot isn't much use.

We took everything out of the cupboard. First the vacuum cleaner, then the feather duster, and then a cardboard box full of broken toys and an old iron which didn't work any more. Then a great pile of newspaper which we saved in case anyone needed it for anything. Right behind the

newspaper we found my lost wellington boot
lying on its side.

I went to push my foot in and I could only get
it halfway. I took my foot out again and looked
inside. 'Oo look!' I said to Francis. 'Someone has
stuffed my boot with tiny torn up scraps of
newspaper.'

Francis looked. 'It wasn't me,' he said.

We showed our Mother. 'Aaah!' she screamed.
'It's a mouse nest!'

'There's nothing wrong with mice,' said
Francis. 'They're nice little creatures and you can
keep them as pets.'

'That's in cages, where they can be kept clean,' answered our Mother. 'Mice spread a good many germs.'

We took the wellington boot out into the garden and carefully tipped the chewed up newspaper onto another sheet of newspaper. It was bitterly disappointing. There wasn't a single mouse to be found in the wellington boot. Not even a baby one. They had grown up and moved out of their special snug little home.

We put the chewed paper in the dustbin and took the boot indoors for our Mother to clean. She stood the boot outside the back door filled to the brim with sudsy water. The rain splashed into it making suds run down the side.

When we went to the shops I had to wear shoes instead of my wellington boots.

Francis walked through the puddles, jumped over some and jumped right into others. I had to walk along with Mother being very sensible and trying to keep my feet out of the worst of the wet.

'When we've grown out of our wellington boots,' said Francis, 'we could keep them for mice to live in.'

'Oh no we couldn't,' answered our Mother. 'Tame mice to keep as pets are quite different, and don't you think we have enough to do already with a tortoise, a dog and a stray cat to care for?'

That afternoon our Mother tidied up the cupboard under the stairs. We helped by moving things and throwing real rubbish into the dustbin. Francis was very pleased. He found a broken car amongst the broken toys, and he thought of a way to mend it which made it useful again.

After that I always looked carefully inside my wellingtons before I put them on, because I didn't want to crush any families of baby mice. I never found any mice or any nests. Once I found a spider which I tipped out into the garden. I didn't think spiders would make very good pets, so I let him run away – which probably made him very happy.

About the Big Gypsy Boy called Musha?

Musha was a big gypsy boy who was almost grown-up. He had left school but he didn't go to work. When children saw him passing in the street they crossed the road and looked the other way. They whispered to each other saying he stole things and started fights.

Musha was the eldest of a large family of gypsy children who went to our school. We stayed away from all the gypsy children and held our noses when we passed one of them – just to let them know we all thought they smelled nasty.

Musha lived with his brothers and sisters in an old cottage behind the school, in the road which led up to the park. We didn't often meet any of them in the park, so that was all right.

Then one day I made friends with Musha, and this is how it happened.

My mother sent me with a message to my aunt.

It was a long way, so my mother said I could ride my bike providing I promised to remember to put out my left hand when I was going to turn left and my right hand when I was going to turn right. That seemed an easy promise to make, so I set off, being careful to put the note for my aunt into my pocket first.

I hurtled through the park on my bike and went bumpety bump along the road where Musha and the gypsy children lived. For what seemed to be no reason at all I suddenly crashed, right outside the gypsy house. Masses of grit went into my knee and a pedal fell off the bike. As everyone knows you can't pedal a bike with only

one pedal. I sat in the middle of the road wiping my knee and wondering what to do. It was no use crying because there was no-one to see.

To my horror Musha came out of his house. He picked up my bike, and I thought he was going to steal it (everyone said he stole things). 'Don't touch that bike, it's mine,' I shouted.

'Hang on, Nipper,' answered Musha, 'I'll see if I can mend it.' He turned the bike upside-down just as they do in bicycle repair shops and tried to fit the fallen pedal back.

I didn't like being called 'Nipper' and I didn't like Musha touching my bike, but there didn't seem to be anything I could do about it without starting a fight. I remembered what my Father had said about keeping out of trouble – so I just waited to see what would happen. I had picked most of the grit out of my knee by this time.

Musha tried to straighten the front wheel but it wouldn't go straight. He tried to fix the pedal back but the bolt was snapped off. The wheels didn't go round, and the bike didn't work at all.

'Where do you live, Nipper?' asked Musha. I told him where I lived. 'O.K. I'd better carry your bike home for you, you won't be able to manage it yourself.'

With that he lifted my bike over his shoulder and headed up the road in the direction of the park and my house. I followed along carrying the

pedal. We chatted all the way – mostly about bikes and living by the park. I rang the door-bell and waited. My Mother was shocked when she saw my knee and the broken bike. She thanked Musha for carrying the bike all the way home for me. 'That's all right Missis,' answered Musha. 'I thought it might get stolen otherwise.'

'That was very kind of Musha,' my Mother said after he had gone. 'Perhaps he's a better lad than everyone makes out. We really shouldn't believe all the gossip we hear about people, should we?'

After that, whenever I saw Musha, he would yell, 'Wotcha Nipper, mind how you go on yer bike.' And I would shout back, 'Wotcha Musha!'

After that I stopped walking past the gypsy children holding my nose. They didn't really smell and it's horrible to be unkind just because everyone else thinks it's funny.

About the Burned and Rusty Scissors?

I remember very well the first time I saw the word 'scissors' printed in a story book. I saw it in the story of The Little Red Hen. I stopped when I came to the word *'scissors'* and I thought to myself, 'That looks strange. It doesn't look anything like it sounds.' And because it looked strange, and because I had stopped to take a long look at the word, I always knew how to spell 'scissors' after that.

We always had trouble in our house with pairs of scissors, and once we had trouble at our Grandmother's house too. One day when we were there I found a piece of wire lying on Grandmother's garden path. I decided to cut it up to make some legs for dollshouse furniture. I searched through several drawers until I found a pair of scissors and then I cut up the wire. I put all the pieces into my pocket to take home. I knew our Grandmother wouldn't have any old cotton reels or matchboxes for making dollshouse furniture. She always threw things away as soon as she had finished with them, even when they might be useful for someone else. Afterwards I put the scissors back where I had found them because people always seem to shout if the scissors get lost.

Later on that day our Grandfather was using the scissors and trying to cut something out of the newspaper. He shouted with rage at our Grandmother, 'These scissors are useless, they

are quite blunt, they won't even cut newspaper.'

I knew he was wrong. I showed him all the tiny pieces of wire I had cut up with the very same scissors. If they could cut through wire I was sure the scissors would cut through thin newspaper and I told him so.

'You've made them blunt cutting the wire,' bellowed our Grandfather like an angry old dragon. And then our Grandmother shouted lots of angry things. After that I was careful to use sewing scissors only for threads and fabrics and paper scissors just for paper.

My brother Francis wasn't so careful. One day we were busy in the garden trying to make a Guy

Fawkes to put on top of our bonfire. Our Mother wouldn't lend us her large and very sharp sewing scissors, in case we made them blunt.

We needed to cut some stiff, thick material. We both hacked away with our paper scissors, trying with both our right and left hands until the insides of our thumbs were bright red and sore.

At last Francis threw down his scissors and said, 'This is useless, I'm going to borrow the sharp sewing scissors for just a moment.' And that was what he did. So we soon finished making the Guy Fawkes. Then we couldn't find the large sharp sewing scissors to put them away. We both hunted high and low but they were nowhere to be seen.

When it was time we burned the Guy Fawkes on top of the bonfire, and very well he blazed too. By then we had forgotten about the lost scissors and our Mother hadn't missed them.

Suddenly one day everyone was shouting at each other about the lost sewing scissors. We had both completely forgotten about borrowing them. Our Mother was very angry – she was certain one of us had borrowed them and forgotten to put them back. Finally she went to the shops in a rage and bought a new pair.

It was about a year later when our Father found the lost scissors. He dug them up in the garden right on the spot where our bonfire had been. He brought them indoors to show us. They were red and rusty from the rain and blue from being burned in the fire.

'No great harm done,' said our Mother, 'I lost them a long time ago and I have a splendid new pair now.'

Francis shuffled and looked at his feet. I could see he remembered borrowing the scissors without asking. Our Father laughed. 'They must have been sewn up inside the Guy Fawkes. Francis, I hope you will never grow up to be a surgeon.' It was a strange thing to say, and at the time I couldn't think why Francis would make a bad surgeon. Still it was probably lucky for everyone that he grew up to be something else. It would be uncomfortable for people to walk about with pairs of sharp scissors and other surgeon's instruments rattling about inside them.